This Oscar book belongs to:

....

....

First published 2006 by Walker Books Ltd
87 Vauxhall Walk, London SE11 5HJ

This edition including DVD published 2008

10 9 8 7 6 5 4 3 2 1

© 2006 Geoff Waring

The right of Geoff Waring to be identified as
author/illustrator of this work has been asserted by him in
accordance with the Copyright, Designs and Patents Act 1988

This book has been typeset in ITCKabel

Printed in China

British Library Cataloguing in Publication Data:
a catalogue record for this book is available from the British Library

ISBN: 978-1-4063-1483-0

www.walkerbooks.co.uk

WALKER BOOKS
AND SUBSIDIARIES
LONDON · BOSTON · SYDNEY · AUCKLAND

For Poppy and Finn
G.W.

The author and publisher would like to thank Sue Ellis at
the Centre for Literacy in Primary Education and Martin Jenkins
for their invaluable input and guidance during the making of this book.

OSCAR
and the
FROG

A BOOK ABOUT GROWING

Geoff Waring

6

One spring day, by the pond, Oscar saw some creatures he had not seen before. Frog hopped up.

"They're tadpoles," he said.

"I was a tadpole before I grew up."

Oscar stared at Frog. He didn't look like a tadpole at all.

"Don't be silly, Frog!" he laughed.

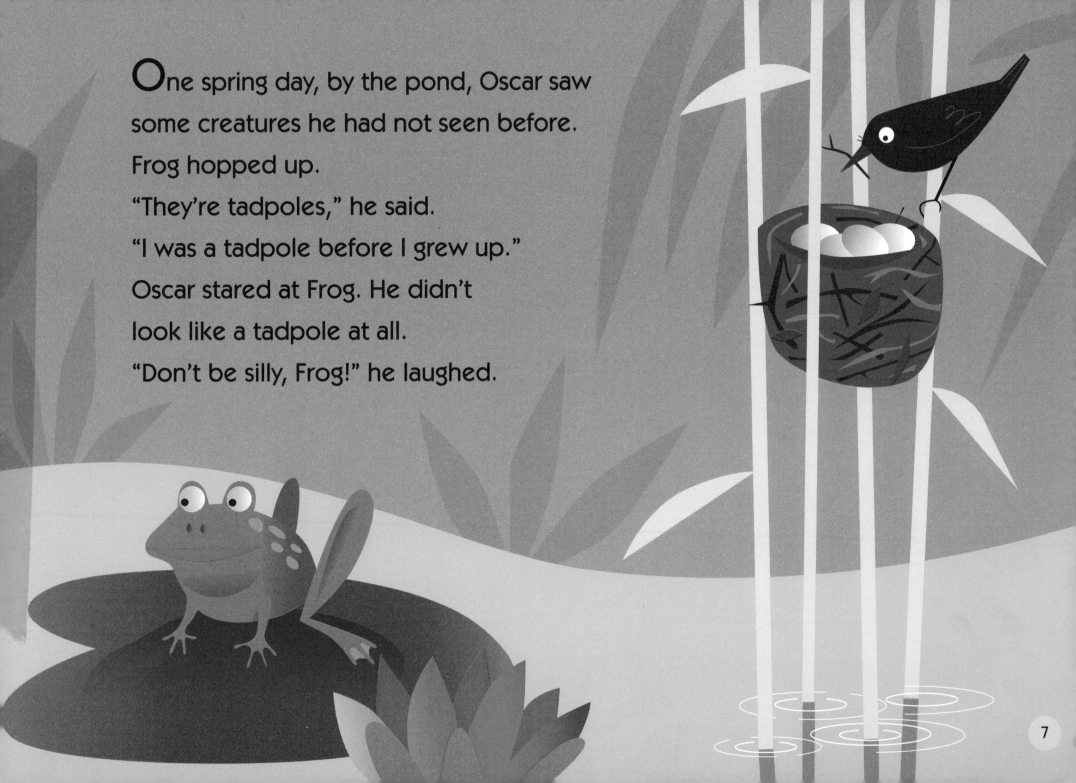

"It's true," Frog said, and he told Oscar how frogs grow.

"At first I looked like a dot in an egg. The egg was as soft as jelly...

I grew in the egg, and hatched out as a wriggly tadpole.

I could breathe under water through "gills" like a fish.

I was hungry for pond weed – it helped me to grow.

Later my gills disappeared as I grew lungs to breathe air with. I grew back legs,

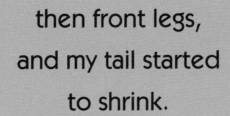

then front legs, and my tail started to shrink.

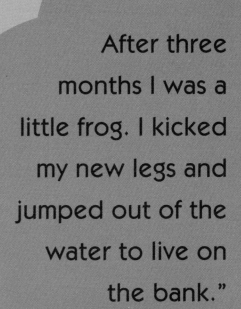

After three months I was a little frog. I kicked my new legs and jumped out of the water to live on the bank."

"What else hatches out of eggs?" Oscar asked. They looked in the pond. Frog showed Oscar some eggs that are laid in water.

Many water snails lay their eggs in pouches of jelly on stones or plants.

Dragonflies often lay their eggs on a plant stem just below the water.

Fish lay lots of eggs. The perch winds hers in long threads around plants, twigs or stones.

11

They looked on the bank and Frog showed Oscar some eggs that are laid where it's dry.

Many kinds of butterfly lay their eggs on the undersides of leaves. When the caterpillars hatch out of the eggs, they will eat the leaves.

Many birds nest high off the ground. Here they are safe from animals who might want to eat their chicks when they hatch.

Ducks often nest on the ground close to water, so their ducklings will be able to swim quickly away from danger.

13

"Do plants hatch out of eggs?" Oscar asked.
"No," said Frog. "Most plants sprout
from seeds. Each plant makes its
own kind of seed."

The seeds of apple trees
are stored inside their fruit.

Strawberry plants have small
seeds on the outsides
of their fruit.

Poppy plants have tiny seeds. They are light enough to be carried in the air.

Coconut palm trees have huge seeds. They can float.

Most seeds ripen above the ground. The seeds of the peanut plant grow in the earth.

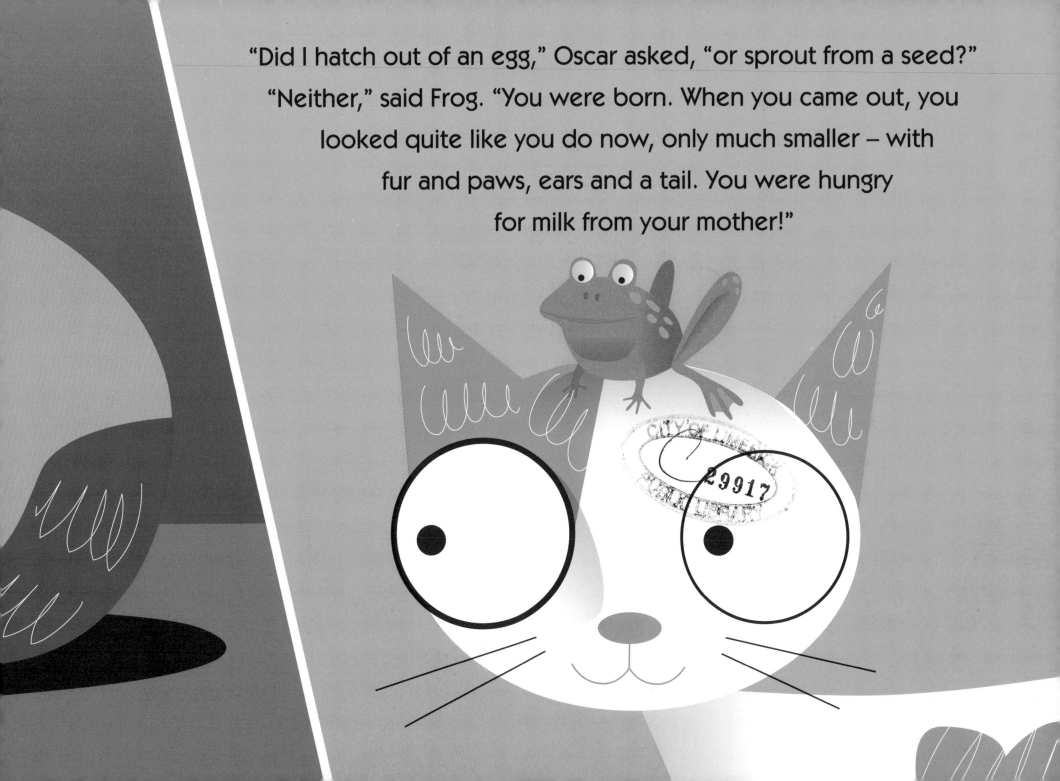

"Did I hatch out of an egg," Oscar asked, "or sprout from a seed?"
"Neither," said Frog. "You were born. When you came out, you looked quite like you do now, only much smaller – with fur and paws, ears and a tail. You were hungry for milk from your mother!"

"Why was I hungry for milk?" Oscar asked.

"It helped you to grow," said Frog.

"Milk for you, pond weed for me ...

leaves for these

caterpillars ...

OSCAR and the FROG
A BOOK ABOUT GROWING

Geoff Waring

OSCAR and the MOTH
A BOOK ABOUT
LIGHT AND DARK

Geoff Waring

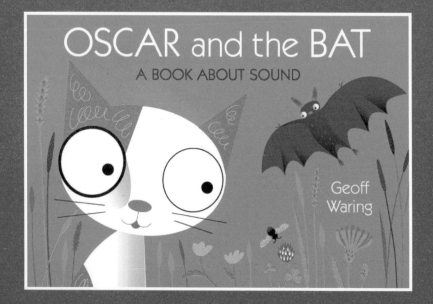

OSCAR and the BAT
A BOOK ABOUT SOUND

Geoff Waring

OSCAR and the CRICKET
A BOOK ABOUT MOVING
AND ROLLING

Geoff Waring

Which of these Oscar books have you read?